Welcome to Rider Nation!

The ALWAYS Team
The Search for Rider Nation

Written by Holly Preston
Illustrated by Val Lawton

Always  Books

The Always Team: The Search for Rider Nation

Text © 2013 Holly Preston
Illustrations © 2013 Val Lawton

Manufactured by Friesens Corporation in Altona, MB, Canada.
June 2013
Job # 83681

Cataloguing data available from Library and Archives Canada.
ISBN: 978-0-9869244-2-2

Editing and layout by Heather Nickel.

With many thanks to the Saskatchewan Roughriders for their cooperation and support.

www.thealwaysteam.com

For all young Rider fans who will ALWAYS
belong to Rider Nation.

Ethan's parents said he was born in Saskatchewan.

He **ALWAYS** believed he'd been born in Rider Nation.

The evidence was everywhere.

Ethan had **ALWAYS** wanted to play football. When he turned seven
he was finally old enough to play on the neighbourhood team
with Stevie, Rob and J.S.

And old enough to ask, "Where IS Rider Nation?"
"You're a smart kid. Figure it out," said Rob, who already knew.
So Ethan decided he would.

Ethan knew just where to go for help.
The search for Rider Nation had begun …

"Just follow your Rider Pride," the big gopher said.

Gordie and Toddy came along to help. The more eyes the better on this mission to find a sign — any sign — that Rider Nation really existed.

"Yes, it's here!" said Ethan when they reached their first town.
Gainer just smiled. As **ALWAYS**, Gordie and Toddy barked their approval.

"Let's take our search to the skies," Ethan said next. The Land of Living Skies spread out below them. "It looks like it's here, too," he said.

"As **ALWAYS**," Gainer agreed.

Then a big Saskatchewan wind blew them far away. "I'm pretty sure Rider Nation is even *here*," Ethan said, as they landed with a bump in the forest.

"Time to ground this search," he added. Gordie and Toddy couldn't have agreed more. And they couldn't believe what they saw next.
*It's **ALWAYS** good to be home,* Gainer thought.

Suddenly Gainer said, "Follow that truck!"

But before they could get any further …

… Ethan proclaimed, "It's time to set sail!"

The little team had covered a lot of ground — on land, in the air and on the water. The signs of Rider Nation were *everywhere* and they weren't finished yet.

"It's **ALWAYS** here," said a firefighter.

"And you'll **ALWAYS** find it here," said a doctor.

"We **ALWAYS** show our Rider Pride," said a baker.

"And it tastes great!" said Gainer.

"Rider Nation is **ALWAYS** alive and well at our place," said a barber.
Gainer thought he should try a new hairstyle.

"Rider Nation **ALWAYS** shops here," said a lady at the grocery store.

"Can I help?" a Rider player asked.

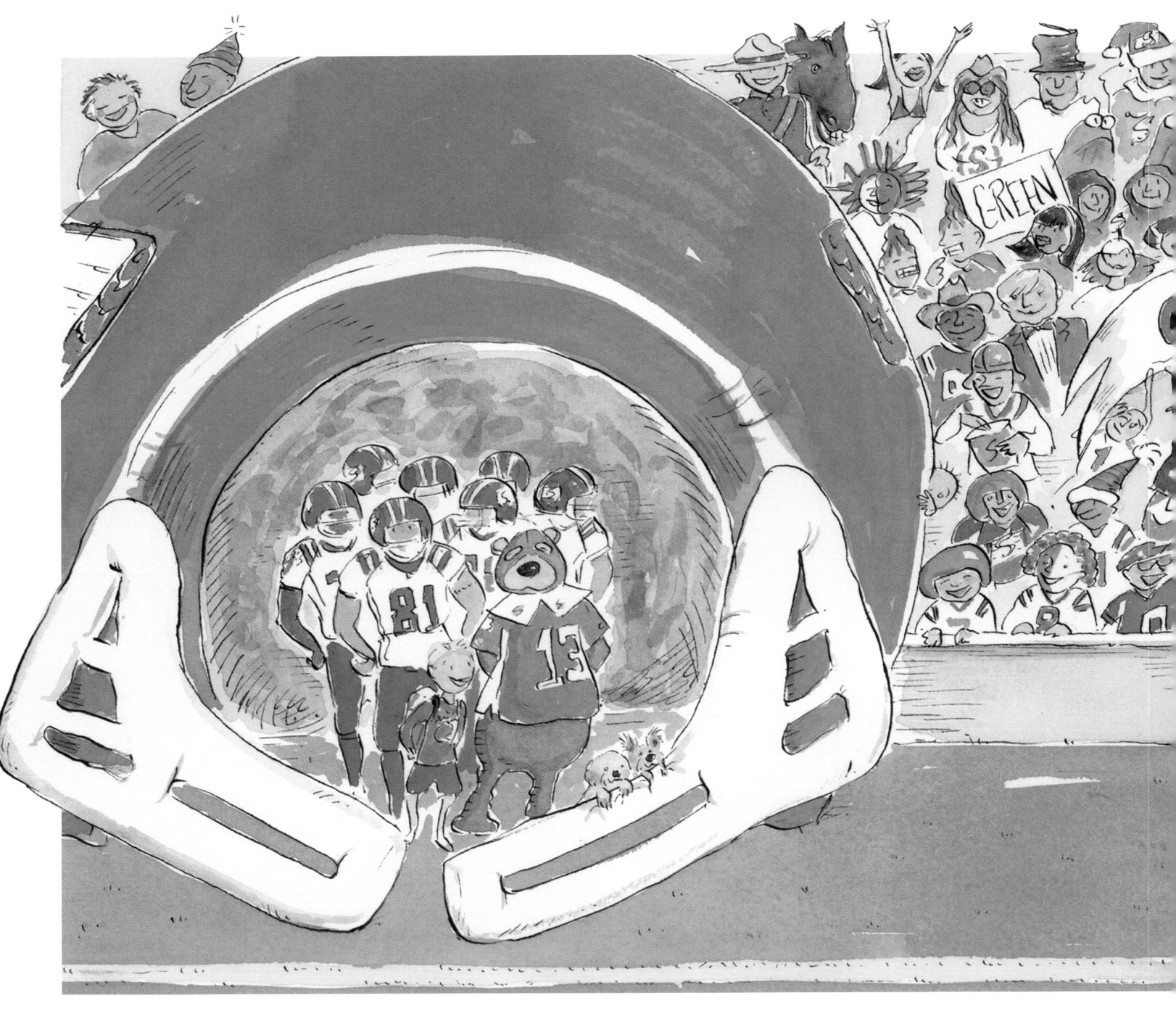

"If you're searching for Rider Nation and you follow your Rider Pride …

… it will **ALWAYS** bring you here!"

"This has been the easiest search ever!" said a very excited Ethan.
"Gainer, now I know — wherever the wheat grows, wherever the wind blows
and wherever the sky is blue — that's **ALWAYS** Rider Nation to me and you!"

Rob, Stevie and J.S. were eager to hear if Ethan had succeeded in his search for Rider Nation. And they could hardly wait to tell him …

… the adventure had just begun!

Holly Preston

Holly has been a Rider fan since way back when. Thankfully, her parents raised her in a place where green and white and community are words that ALWAYS belong in the same sentence.

She has had a career as a broadcast journalist with CTV and CBC and currently hosts a daily CBC radio program.. On the day our team brought the Grey Cup home in 1989, she was lucky to host a TV special from Taylor Field watched by fans throughout Saskatchewan. It's the only time she'll ever get to be on the 50-yard line. How sweet it was!

Today, Holly's two sons wear their Rider colours with pride, just as their grandfathers Ken and Ted would want.

Val Lawton

When you're a little girl growing up on the golden prairies of Saskatchewan, your dreams are as big as the endless swaying wheat fields and the eternal blue sky stretching overhead. For Val, those dreams were filled with simple yet compelling images of people dotted against a landscape washed with sun.

Val's favourite books as a kid always had great pictures—like Winnie-the-Pooh, *and* Tim and Lucy Go to Sea. *It was the books with the simple, scratchy drawings that let her imagination run wild. So when it came to drawing her own pictures, she followed in the footsteps of illustrators like Ernest Shepard and Edward Ardizzone.* The Search for Rider Nation *is her 19th book.*

Val lives with a husband, two kids and two beagles, all of whom cheer for the ALWAYS Team on game day!